The Village

Lily Pad Pond

Buttercup Cottage

Hardwick House

Purdey's Pasture

River Noodle

For P. J. – the true inspiration for Little Red
—S. F.

For Iris and Robert, with love
—S. W.

SIMON AND SCHUSTER

First published in Great Britain in 2006 by Simon & Schuster UK Ltd
Africa House, 64-78 Kingsway, London WC2B 6AH

Published in the USA in 2006 by Simon & Schuster Books for Young Readers, an imprint of
Simon & Schuster Children's Publishing Division, New York

This paperback edition first published 2007

Book design by David Bennett
The text for this book is set in Goudy
The illustrations for this book are rendered in soft pencil and watercolour on Arches paper

A CIP catalogue record for this book is available from the British Library upon request

ISBN-13 9780689875717
ISBN-10 0689875711

Printed in China
1 3 5 7 9 10 8 6 4 2

Little Red's
Summer Adventure

Sarah Ferguson
The Duchess of York

Illustrated by
Sam Williams

SIMON AND SCHUSTER

London   New York   Sydney

*I*t was a sizzling hot summer's day at Buttercup Cottage.
Butterflies fluttered and bees buzzed busily amongst the daisies and
the clover. Gino ran between Little Red and Little Blue, wagging
his tail as usual, and barking happily.

"I'm just so excited!" cried Little Blue as he jumped from foot to
foot. "The River Noodle Boating Bonanza is always so much fun.
What a buzz of a day!"

Roany stood by the Wonky Wooden Wagon.

"Do we have to go?" she asked grumpily. "I always end up giving pony rides and it's just too hot! I want to stay in the shade."

"Giddy up!" said Little Red cheerfully. "You know how much everyone loves your rides – you're the star attraction." She plopped a floppy hat on Roany's head. "This will keep you cool!" she said.

Roany smiled out of the corner of her mouth. She was secretly pleased about being so popular.

"Alright then," she snorted, "so long as I have an enormous bucket of iced carrot juice to drink."

They hadn't gone far when, all of a sudden, a great pigeon crashed and skidded onto the roof of the Wonky Wooden Wagon.

"I really must practise my landings," he said.

"Blakesley Bill!" guffawed Roany, happy to see her old friend. "I knew you'd come."

"Wouldn't miss the River Noodle Boating Bonanza for the world," chuckled Blakesley Bill. "What's the prize for the winning boat this year?"

"A chance to turn the magic key on the Wonky Wooden Wagon," said Little Red.

"So that it turns into a supersummertastic surprise!" interrupted Little Blue, jumping up and down.

Just then the Wonky Wooden Wagon
trundled around a bend in the lane and
the River Noodle came into view . . .

. . . and what an amazing sight it was!
"Jumping jellybeans!" exclaimed
Little Blue as he looked on in awe.
Little Red was speechless – the river
had never looked so beautiful.

Purdey pranced busily by the boathouse. "I've made heaps of juicy jelly-baby jelly, marvellous marshmallow meringues and whipped watermelon ice-cream," she said proudly. "I just need some help to push the Jelly Boat into the water – it's going to be a floating, boating sweetie bar!"

"Scrumtumlicious!" said Little Blue, smacking his lips together. "Look, we've brought these balloons and streamers to decorate the boathouse."

Little Red delved into the box of paper hats and
started to hand them to all of the contestants. Then
she called for them all to climb aboard their boats.

"I love the badgers' painted wheelbarrow, and the squirrels' watering can is beautifully polished," she whispered to Bear, "but the robins look so pretty in their little teacup, and don't the rabbits look dandy in their old boot, too!"

"What do you think of our Hardwick House gravy boat?" called Mole.

"Surely the prize is ours!" added Vole.

"Let's just wait and see!" replied Little Red kindly. "Oh look, the field mice have really gone to town with their cheeseboard – what a clever idea. And my goodness, a boat full of holes!" giggled Little Red. "How are you going to keep afloat?"

"Ladles!" spluttered Duck and Goose, baling out frantically.

"How on earth are you going to decide who wins?" puzzled Little Blue.

"I'll have a careful think while we go over to see how Roany's getting on," replied Little Red.

"Roll up! Roll up!" chirped Blakesley Bill, helping a group of frogs onto Roany's back.

"Laughing leapfrogs!" croaked the littlest frog. "I could never jump this high. I can even see Hardwick House!"

"Is everything tickety-boo?" asked Little Red.

"I suppose so," muttered Roany, "but surely it must be time for a break." Little Red carried over a bucket of ice-cold carrot juice.

"Have a good, long sip and a quick kip while I announce the Boating Bonanza winners," she said as she nuzzled Roany's muzzle.

Little Blue honked his horn loudly and at once there was hush.
The only sound came from the whispering waters of the River Noodle.

"This year the boats are more spectacular than ever!" announced
Little Red.

"But there has to be a winner and I've decided that the prize
should go to . . . the rabbits!"

"Hurrah! Hooray! Whoopee!" everyone cried and clapped.

Little Red carried the baby rabbits up the ladder so that they could scamper onto the roof. But, just as they were about to turn the key . . .

… a magpie swooped down and snatched it clean away!

"Oh, you naughty, nasty nuisance!" exclaimed Little Red as the magpie soared into the sky.

But the key was too heavy for the magpie and it fell into the River Noodle with a huge SPLOSH!

"Coconut carumbers!" shrieked Little Blue as he ran to the water's edge. "We'll never find the key now!"

At that moment, Mr Ron Bow popped his head out of the water. "Hello, everybody!" he said. "You'll never guess what just happened. There I was, swimming along, minding my own business, when – out of nowhere – an enormous key boffed me on the end of the nose!"

"I'm so sorry," said Little Red. "It's the key to our Wonky Wooden Wagon but a very naughty magpie just stole it. Is there any chance you could get it for us?"

"Okay, lass, I'll do my best!" said Mr Ron Bow, giving a quick salute and diving beneath the surface. Moments later he popped up again.

"Terribly sorry, my dear," he puffed. "What did you just ask me to do? You know us trout. Memories like goldfish!"

"The key…" began Little Red.

"Of course, silly me!" apologised the trout. "Won't be a tick!" and with that he splashed back into the river. And then back up again!

"I hate to be a nuisance," he spluttered, "but if you could just remind me…"

"Oh dear," said Little Red. "I think we're going to need someone else's help here!

As quick as a flash, Little Red reached into her Sack of Smiles and took out her magic bubble blower. She began to blow tiny rainbow-coloured bubbles all over Gino's fur.

All of a sudden with a fizz, pop, flash, bang, wallop,
Gino turned into…

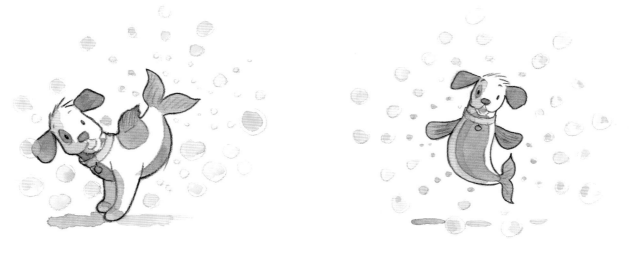

… a dogfish! In one graceful movement he dived
into the River Noodle.

Down,
      down,
            down he doggy-paddled. Past forgetful
Mr Ron Bow. Past a winking, whiskery catfish. Gino
was desperate to give chase but knew he was on a very
important mission and kept on swimming.

Suddenly he saw the golden magic key, half buried
in the riverbed. Gino flicked it free with his tail.

"Bravo!" shouted the crayfish, who were watching
in amazement.

With a triumphant splash, Gino leapt
out of the water, dropping the key at
Little Red's feet.

"Well, blow me down with a feather!"
exclaimed Blakesley Bill.

"Fishtastic!" cried Little Blue, as he
cartwheeled round in circles

Gino shook himself dry and back into
his doggy shape.

"Woof, woof!" he barked. He was happy
to have a tail to wag again.

"Gino, you're a hero!" cheered Little
Red, and she kissed his head. "And now,"
she said to everyone, "the little rabbits
shall turn the magic key on the Wonky
Wooden Wagon."

"I'll circle overhead to make sure that
naughty magpie doesn't come back," said
Blakesley Bill as he prepared for take-off.

"Let the surprise now start before our eyes!" announced Little Red.

With a puff of smoke . . .

a whiz and a whirl . . .

a **clutter** and
a **clatter** . . .

and a flicker of tiny fairy lights . . .

the wagon turned into
the most beautiful
carousel. Each one of the
brightly painted horses
looked just like Roany!

"Splendiferous!" cried Little Blue.

"WOW!" everyone gasped as they climbed onto the little horses. The sun was beginning to set as the carousel spun round and round and the River Noodle looked even more magical than ever.

"Thank you, everyone, for such a wonderful day," said Little Red. "I think this has been the best Boating Bonanza ever!"

The Village

Buttercup Cottage

Lily Pad Pond

Hardwick House

Purdey's Pasture

River Noodle